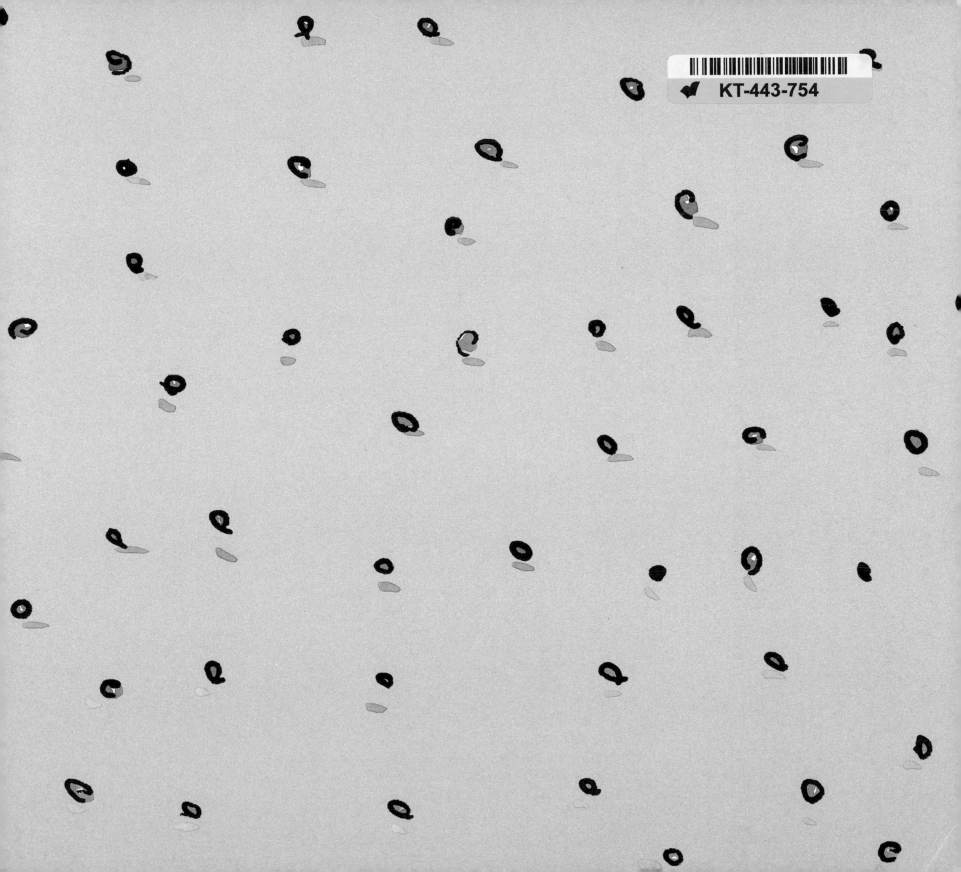

TO NATASHA, WHO LIKES CHIPS BEST!

First published 2002 by Walker Books Ltd
87 Vauxhall Walk, London SE11 5HJ

This edition published 2003

4 6 8 10 9 7 5 3

© 2002 Charlotte Voake

The right of Charlotte Voake to be identified as author/illustrator
of this work has been asserted by her in accordance with the
Copyright, Designs and Patents Act 1988

This book has been typeset in Godlike

Printed in China

British Library Cataloguing in Publication Data:
a catalogue record for this book is available
from the British Library

ISBN 0-7445-9810-9

# Pizza Kittens

## Charlotte Voake

**WALKER BOOKS**
AND SUBSIDIARIES
LONDON · BOSTON · SYDNEY

"It's teatime," said Mum.
"Fish fingers – your
favourite!"
"Not *my*
favourite,"
said Joe.
"I wanted
baked beans."

"I like pizza," said Lucy.

 "Ooh, pizza," said Bert.

"We all like
PIZZA best!"

"I'm giving you
lettuce too," said Mum.

"Oh no, not lettuce!"
they cried.

Lucy, Joe and Bert only stayed at the table for five minutes and this was how they left it.

What a horrible sight
it was!

"Stop right there!"
said Mum.
"Look at
this mess!
Lettuce
all over
the floor!"

"That's it!" said Dad. "Tomorrow we will all eat together, you will eat your food, and you will try to be helpful."

The next evening began well.
"This is going to be delicious, though
I say so myself," said Dad.
"Shall we lay
the table, Dad?"
asked Joe.

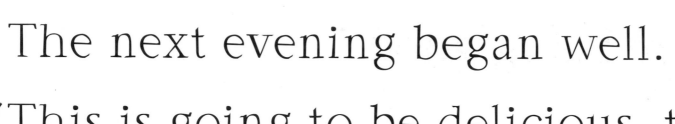

"You *are* being good," said Mum.

"Isn't this nice," said Mum. "All of us sitting down together."

"Ooh, is it lemonade?" asked Joe when Mum came back with the drinks. "No, it's water," said Mum.

"I wanted orange juice," said Lucy.

"I don't really like water," said Bert.

"OH NO! NOT PEAS!"
said Joe, Lucy and Bert.
"We *really* don't
like PEAS!"

"Don't put so much ketchup on them," said Mum to Joe and Lucy. "And please try to look a bit happier."

"I'm looking forward to this," said Dad. "Turn round, Bert. Then we can all START!"

"Ohhhhh!" said Bert. "Ohh..."

"Quick!" said Dad.

"Quick, get a cloth!"

"I'll get it!" said Lucy.

"I'll go!" said Joe.

"NO!" said Mum.

"Please! Let's all just
SIT DOWN
and
EAT UP!"

"But it's all COLD," said Joe, "and Bert's peas are swimming in water!"

"Well," said Mum, when Joe, Lucy and Bert were getting ready for bed, "that wasn't very good, was it?

Dad's still clearing up the mess;
peas *everywhere*!"

"Sorry, Mum," said Lucy and Joe.

"I didn't mean
to spill my
drink," said Bert.

"I know you
didn't," said Mum.

"We'll try again tomorrow."

The next night Mum said, "Dad's making us something *lovely* for tea."

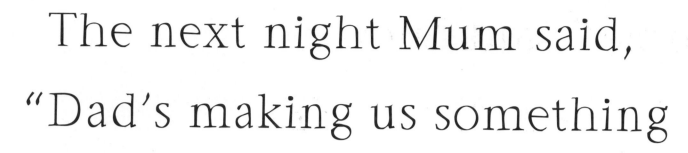

"Is it peas?" said Joe.

"No," said Mum. "Dad's gone right off peas!"

"Is it chips?" said Lucy.

"No," said Dad. "It's PIZZA!"

"Ooh!" said Joe, Lucy and Bert. "Our *favourite!*"

"You're a brilliant cook, Dad," said Joe.

"Thank you!" said Dad.

"This," said Mum, "is absolutely perfect!"

"Yes!" said Bert...

"Absolutely
PERFECT!"

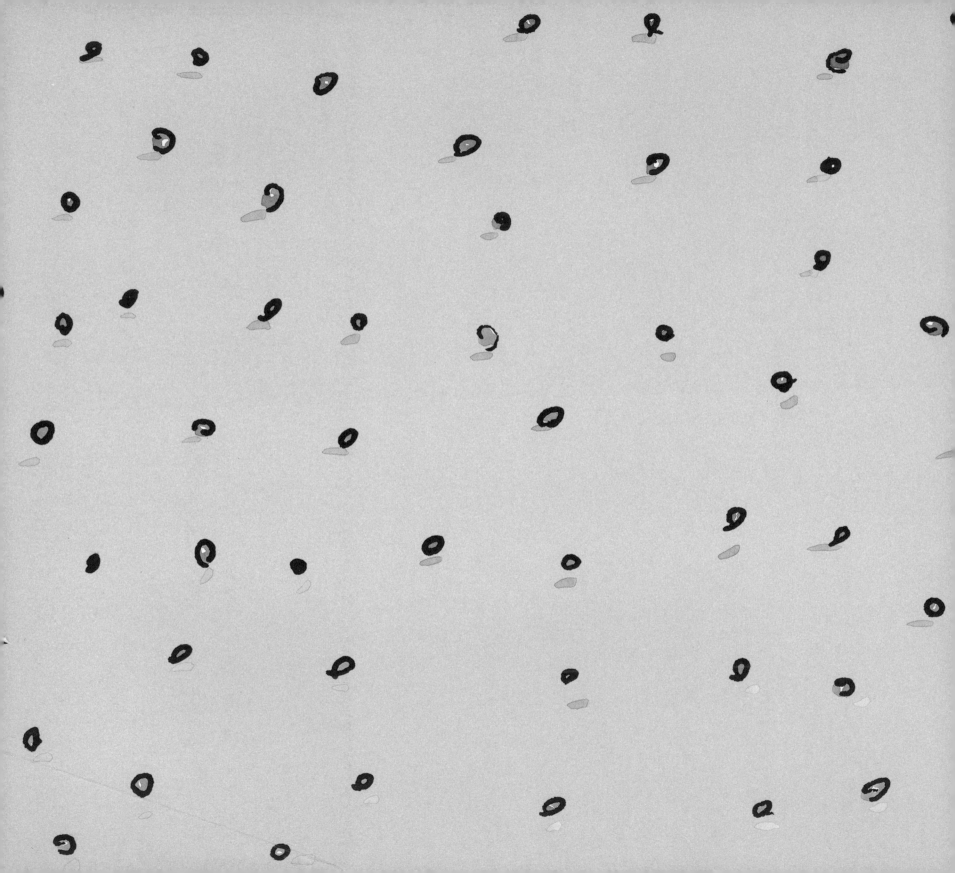

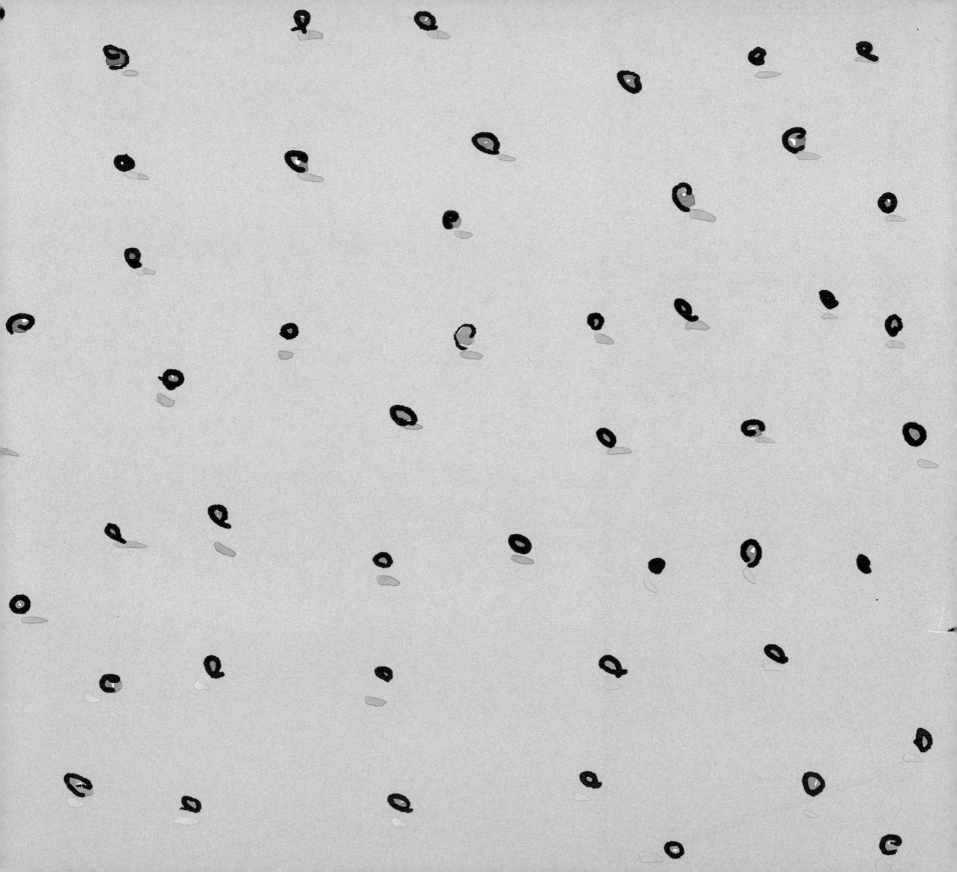